Call of the Wild

I0614943

Grades 7-8

Written by Margot Southall
Illustrated by Laurie Stevens

ISBN 1-55035-355-1
Copyright 1996
Revised January 2006
All Rights Reserved * Printed in Canada

Published in the United States by:
On the Mark Press
3909 Witmer Road PMB 175
Niagara Falls, New York
14305
www.onthemarkpress.com

Published in Canada by:
S&S Learning Materials
15 Dairy Avenue
Napanee, Ontario
K7R 1M4
www.sslearning.com

Look For Other Intermediate - Novel Studies

The Call of the Wild

By Jack London

Table of Contents

The
Call of the Wild

By Jack London

Expectations

1. To introduce students to the literary genre of the author Jack London.

2. To demonstrate the bond, respect and friendship that can be obtained between a man and an animal.

3. To show how one can endure and overcome cruel and difficult adversities in one's life.

4. To make students more aware of the climate, location and geographical aspects of the Yukon, a territory found in Canada.

5. To acquaint students with the hardships, dangers met and lifestyles of people during the Gold Rush on the Klondike River in the Yukon.

Synopsis of the Story

The Call of the Wild

"The Call of the Wild" follows the life of a domestic dog who is taken from his comfortable home to become a sled dog in the wilds of the Yukon Territory. This is the time of the Klondike Gold Rush and heavy, strong dogs are in demand. Buck has reigned supreme at Judge Miller's place in Santa Clara Valley for the past four years. His father was a St. Bernard, his mother a Scotch Shepherd. At 140 pounds, Buck is fit from hunting and cold-tubbing races. Manuel, Judge Miller's gardener, is short of money, so he dognaps Buck and sells him. Now Buck's life has changed forever. He finds himself on a train bound for San Francisco where the "dog-breaker" clubs him into submission. This vicious treatment introduces Buck to "the reign of primitive law". Buck now has a different perspective on life and the "latent cunning of his nature" is aroused. He recognizes that "a man with a club was a lawgiver, a master to be obeyed, but not necessarily conciliated." Buck is put aboard the Narwhal bound for the Klondike. En route he is purchased by a French Canadian, Perrault. On arrival, he has his first puzzling experience with snow.

Buck now begins his training as a sled dog and quickly learns to meet the expectations of his team. He learns how to survive through cunning, opportunism and "an internal and external economy." Buck soon adapts to the law of club and fang and becomes skilled at the wolf-like manner of fighting. This harsh environment brings to life the "wilder instincts" within him and Buck begins his response to the "call of the wild".

The Call of the Wild

By Jack London

Buck suffers a series of hardships as a sled dog at the mercy of both fair and cruel masters. Finally, he is rescued from near death by John Thornton, a man Buck comes to love with a passionate loyalty. Buck proves his love for Thornton again and again as they share a number of intense experiences. But, even though he is happy with his life with Thornton, he never forgets his "wilder nature" and is beckoned by a parallel world of wolves and the collective memories of his ancestors.

When Thornton is killed by the Yeehats, the final tie to a domestic existence is broken and Buck's answer to the "Call" becomes complete. Buck becomes the feared "ghost dog" of the valley and assumes his rightful role as leader of the wolf pack.

Author Biography

Jack London

Jack London was not only a writer, he was also an adventurer. He was born in San Francisco in 1876, but grew up in Oakland, California. His family was very poor and when he was a child he helped support them by selling newspapers. At seventeen, he went to sea as a sailor. When he returned he entered a writing contest. His experiences at sea and his talent for writing vivid descriptions enabled him to win first prize. This gave him the confidence to continue writing.

For the next few years he traveled around the United States and Canada. It was at this point that London realized he did not have a direction in his life. So he went back to school and completed his high school courses and one year at the University of California.

When he was twenty-one he spent a year in the Klondike, searching for gold and good stories. It was this experience that provided the motivation for writing "The Call of the Wild" and "White Fang".

During the war between Japan and Russia, London was asked to become a war correspondent. He also reported on the activities of the bandit, Pancho Villa in Mexico. His keen observation skills were of value in both non-fictional and fictional writing.

London never lost his love of the sea. and in 1906 he and his wife sailed around the world in a schooner that he had designed himself. When he returned, he continued writing. Some of the books he wrote were about himself, such as "Martin Eden"; others were about the struggles of the poor, something he knew about firsthand, such as "Iron Heel". His books have been translated into many different languages. In his lifetime he wrote forty-eight books. He died in 1916 at the age of forty.

The
Call of the Wild

By Jack London

Teacher Planning Guide

1. The Chapter Analysis Questions may be completed as a whole or small group activity. Alternatively, you may wish to have students read and work on the Chapter Questions and follow-up activities at their own pace.

2. Answers to the Chapter Questions may be compiled into a student response booklet along with the follow up activities for evaluation.

3. Distribute copies of the Chapter Summary Chart to students and instruct them that they are to complete the chart in point form as they read each chapter under the headings Chapter __, Characters (we meet in this chapter), Events (in order), and the results of these Events.

4. Set up a display area for other books by Jack London, such as "White Fang" and "Sea Wolf". Have students research further details of his biography and discuss what motive he might have gained from his experiences to write "Call of the Wild".

5. Enlist the help of the teacher-librarian to provide materials on the Klondike Gold Rush, Yukon Territory, wolves, moose, Early Man (prehistoric), Native Peoples of the Yukon and the history of the domestication of dogs. Each of these could provide possible research topics for group or independent research.

6. Display a map of the Yukon and use markers, such as small flags to trace the routes Buck covered as a sled dog and later in his adventures with Thornton.

7. Invite a dog trainer or someone who has experience with sled dogs to make a presentation to the class.

8. If this unit is taught in the winter, have a snow fest, with "human" sled races.

9. Show your class a video on dog sled racing, the Yukon, the History of the Klondike Gold Rush or life in Canada at this time.

10. Discuss the topics "instincts" and "emotions". List human and "other animal" instincts and emotions. Compare the positive and negative consequences of these two elements in the story.

11. Encourage a healthy respect for nature. Brainstorm with students and list the natural beauties and dangers in the area where you live.

12. To develop vocabulary in a cooperative learning activity, have small groups of students work on a particular chapter list. Students will research the definition of each word and then illustrate its meaning in a sentence. These may be recorded in chart form and displayed for class reference.

The Call of the Wild

By Jack London

13. Create your own aurora borealis in the classroom. Have students sprinkle several colors of powdered paint on a sheet of white paper. Using a dampened paintbrush, students will then swirl the colors together. When the paper is dry, students may paste silhouettes of black construction paper to represent appropriate northern scenery.

14. Brainstorm and list the many uses of gold in our society. Discuss the possible reasons why people would leave their homes and their families to risk their lives in search of gold. Research other gold rushes such as the ones in California or Australia. Discuss the impact on that area in both human and environmental terms.

15. Jack London was known for his keen observation of nature and his love of the outdoors. Follow his model by taking students on a nature hike to observe and sketch scenes in nature. Alternatively, students could recollect and share memorable scenes. Display student artwork on a bulletin board entitled "The Call of the Wild".

16. Discuss the themes addressed in the novel such as "survival of the fittest" and "even though we are civilized, we all have a primitive side or latent animal instincts".

17. Develop your students' skills in predicting outcomes:
    a) Have students look at the cover and illustrations in the book. Discuss the title, possible characters, settings and events. You may wish to make a list of class predictions and confirm and disconfirm as you read the novel.

    b) Ask students what they would like to find out about Buck, the Yukon and the Klondike Gold Rush. Make a chart of student questions and use this chart as a focus for reading throughout the novel study. Complete the chart as students discover the answers to each question.

Chapter Analysis: Pre-reading Discussion Questions

Chapter One: Into the Primitive

1. What do you think the title "Into the Primitive" could refer to?

2. Jack London participated in the Klondike Gold Rush in 1897. How would this experience affect his perspective in writing this novel? Does it make the story more credible to you?

The Call of the Wild

By Jack London

Chapter Two: The Law of Club and Fang

1. To whom would the club and fang belong?

2. Describe the role this law could play in Buck's life? Why would it be important for him to obey?

3. Explain the consequences of breaking such a law?

Chapter Three: The Dominant Primordial Beast

1. What is Jack London referring to as "the primordial beast"? How does this relate to Buck?

2. What would Buck have to do to become the dominant beast?

Chapter Four: Who Has Won to Mastership

1. When London uses the term "mastership", to what is he referring? Mastership of what?

Chapter Five: The Toil of Trace and Trail

1. Define the terms "toil" and "trace".

2. Focus on the title of this chapter. What could it predict for Buck?

3. Does it sound like a positive or negative future ahead for Buck?

Chapter Six: For the Love of a Man

1. Whose love is London referring to and who is the man receiving it?

2. Why might Buck develop such a love for Thornton?

3. Do you think he was justified in feeling this way? Was Thornton worthy of his love? Describe the character traits that he possessed that could earn Buck's admiration.

Chapter Seven: The Sounding of the Call

1. What "call" is London referring to in the title of this chapter?

2. Why would Buck respond to "the call of the wild" now that he is happy in his life with Thornton? What could happen to cause him to live as a wild animal?

3. How do you think the story will end?

The Call of the Wild

By Jack London

Vocabulary Word List

Chapter One:

artesian
demesne
sated
progeny
conveyance

metamorphosed
ferocity
cayuses
weazened
soliloquized

ruction
conciliated
culprit
incurious
lacerated

Chapter Two:

primordial
vicarious
diabolically
incarnation

ignominously
placatingly
retaliate
fastidious

malingerer
retrogression
cadences

Chapter Three:

pandemonium
dubiously
conspicuous
insubordination
aurora borealis

plaint
covert
mutiny
prostrate
vexation

antagonists
strife
primordial
ecstasy
inexorable

Chapter Four:

obdurate

lugubriously

celerity

Chapter Five:

salient
chaffering
superfluous
innocuously

feigned
remonstrate
voracious
convulsed

callowness
inexorable
perambulating

Chapter Six:

ministrations
manoeuvre

peremptorily

plethoric

Chapter Seven:

commingled
ptarmigan
contagion
excrescence

pertinacity
paroxysms
wantoness
infinitesimal

carnivorous
slake
ambuscade

The
Call of the Wild

By Jack London

List of Skills

The Chapter Analysis Questions cover a variety of skills. These include both comprehension of the information in the novel as well as higher order thinking analysis, prediction, interpretation and evaluation skills.

Vocabulary Development:

1. Definitions: matching definitions to story vocabulary
2. Identifying similes and metaphors
3. Locating descriptive words and phrases
4. Listing antonyms
5. Listing synonyms
6. Using context clues

Setting Activities:

1. Summarizing the details of a setting
2. Create a time chart
3. Listing dangers and survival tips described in the novel
4. Map the route
5. Create a time capsule for 1897
6. Create a story map

Plot Activities:

1. Graph the plot
2. Summarize the plot in a cloze
3. Complete a flow chart of events
4. Create a different ending
5. Analyze cause and effect
6. Represent the main events in a stair chart
7. Complete a story grammar
8. Sequence the events in a countdown
9. Identify conflict in the story

Character Activities:

1. Compare story problems
2. Locate evidence of heroic traits
3. Create a character web
4. Label a literary sociogram
5. Match quotations of story characters

The Call of the Wild

By Jack London

6. Identify character roles
7. Illustrate and describe a character
8. Identify the use of personification
9. Identify and describe a round and a flat character
10. Compare two characters

Creative and Critical Thinking:

1. Research the natural resources of the Yukon
2. Reason paragraph: Life in the wild
3. Choose and expand on an alternative plot line
4. Letter home from the northland
5. Describe survival traits
6. Outline prosecution and defense of a story character
7. Research inventions
8. Create a venn diagram of domesticated and wild dogs
9. Identify Buck's emotions and instincts as a help or hindrance
10. Summarize the story in a news report

Art Activities:

1. Create a travel brochure of the Yukon
2. Illustrate a scene
3. Portrait of Buck
4. Create an Aurora Borealis
5. Cruelty to animals poster
6. Missing dog poster

The
Call of the Wild

By Jack London

Student Activity Tracking Sheet

Put a check mark in the box at the end of each activity that you complete.

Chapter Analysis Questions: ☐

Vocabulary Development:

1. Definitions ☐
2. Similies and Metaphors ☐
3. Descriptive Words and Phrases ☐
4. Opposites ☐
5. Synonyms ☐
6. Context Clues ☐

Setting Activities:

1. Novel Scenes ☐
2. A Time and a Place in History ☐
3. Dangers and Survival Tips ☐
4. Mapping the Route ☐
5. Time Capsule ☐
6. Story Map ☐

Plot Activities:

1. Graphing the Plot ☐
2. Cloze It ☐
3. Resolving Story problems ☐
4. A Different Ending ☐
5. Cause and Effect ☐
6. Plot Development ☐
7. Story Grammar ☐
8. Story Countdown ☐
9. Conflict in the Story ☐

Character Activities:

1. Character Comparison ☐
2. Buck the hero ☐
3. Character Web ☐
4. Literary Sociagram ☐
5. Who Sai It? ☐
6. Character Role ☐
7. Picture Paragraphs ☐
8. Man or Beast ☐
9. Flat or Round Characters ☐
10. Character Comparison ☐

Creative and Critical Thinking:

1. Natural Resources ☐
2. The Wild Side of Life ☐
3. Novel Substitutions ☐
4. Letter from the North ☐
5. Survival of the Fittest ☐
6. Cruelty Against Animals ☐
7. Inventors and Their Inventions ☐
8. Wild, Domesticated or Both? ☐
9. Instincts and Emotions ☐
10. News Story ☐

Art Activities:

1. Travel Brochure ☐
2. Illustrate a Scene ☐
3. Portrait of a Hero ☐
4. Aurora Borealis ☐
5. Cruelty to Animals Poster ☐
6. Missing Dog Poster ☐

The Call of the Wild

By Jack London

Name: _____

The Call of the Wild

By Jack London

Chapter Analysis Questions

(Student Copy)

Chapter One: Into the Primitive

1. In the beginning of the story Jack London uses descriptive phrases to establish the scene at Judge Miller's place. List four descriptive phrases that he used, example: wide-spreading lawns.

2. Jack London creates an image of Buck as a king. Locate evidence of this image on page 10 and 11 and record one description of Buck as King.

3. What breeds of dogs were Buck's mother and father?

4. Which phrase on page 12 best describes Buck's rage at being dognapped?

5. On page 14 London shows us Buck's point of view about the situation. Summarize Buck's perspective on the plight he found himself in.

6. Buck is no longer the same dog. His experiences have changed him forever. Describe the change that has come over Buck on page 15.

7. How is Buck introduced to "the reign of primitive law"?

8. What does London mean when he writes that a man with a club was a lawgiver, a master to be obeyed, though not necessarily conciliated" (page 19)? Why do you think it was necessary for London to portray Buck as a dog who would not conciliate?

9. Perrault becomes Buck's new owner. What character traits or qualities did Perrault possess that earned Buck's respect?

10. Identify three qualities of Buck's that you would have admired. Give reasons for your choices.

Chapter Two: The Law of the Club and Fang

1. Why were there "neither peace, nor rest, nor a moment's safety for Buck on Dyea Beach"?

2. What lesson did Buck learn from the attack on Curly?

3. Why did Buck develop a hatred for Spitz in this chapter?

4. Describe the wolf manner of fighting.

5. How did Buck learn to survive the bitterly cold nights?

6. Notice the human qualities London gives Buck in this chapter. List three of these.

7. Identify the experience Buck has that drives him back to "the lives of his forebears" on page 28.

The Call of the Wild

By Jack London

8. The sled dogs Sol-leks and Dave had two ambitions in life. What were they?

9. Buck soon adapted to the "law of club and fang". Describe the event in this chapter that demonstrated Buck was fit to survive a harsh environment.

10. Why would respecting personal feelings and property and other civilized behavior be a handicap in the North?

11. London describes Buck's "internal and external economy" on page 33. Explain what he means by this phrase.

12. London refers to life as a "puppet thing" on page 34. What do you think he means by this, in terms of Buck's response to the call of the wild?

Chapter Three: The Dominant Primordial Beast

1. Which event finally triggered Buck's attack on Spitz and what postponed the duel?

2. What dangers did the team face crossing the Thirty Mile River and how was Perrault saved?

3. What caused Dolly to "go mad" on page 42?

4. London uses conversations between Francois and Perrault to provide commentary on Buck's character and to predict possible future events. Do you think London's use of phonetic spelling to convey their accent is effective? Give reasons for your statement.

5. Spitz felt his leadership was threatened by Buck. What kind of primitive character traits had Buck developed that posed a threat to Spitz?

6. How did the "pride of toil and trace" transform Dave and Sol-leks?

7. Buck likes to interfere when Spitz has arguments with other dogs. Why do you think London refers to this as "covert mutiny" and what is the effect on the team?

8. On page 48 London describes "an ecstasy that marks the summit of life, and beyond which life cannot rise ... this ecstasy comes when one is most alive, and it comes as a complete forgetfulness that one is alive." This is a time when we are so caught up in the joy of what we are doing, that we are oblivious of all else. Brainstorm and suggest a moment when someone could experience "this forgetfulness of living" other than what is given in the text.

9. At the beginning of Buck's fight with Spitz, the scene of the battle became somehow familiar to Buck? How could this happen?

10. What characteristics of a "practised fighter" did Spitz demonstrate?

11. "Buck possessed a quality that made for greatness" (page 51). What was this quality and how did he use it to win the fight with Spitz and become the "dominant primordial beast"?

The Call of the Wild

By Jack London

Chapter Four: Who has Won to Mastership

1. How does Francois describe Buck? Why?

2. How does Buck react when Francois places Sol-leks in the lead dog position? Explain his reasons for behaving this way.

3. Think about the part of the story where London writes "Buck laughed, as dogs laugh.." How might a dog laugh? What kind of body language would they use to demonstrate their amusement?

4. Decide if Buck's leadership had a positive or negative effect on the team? Give an example from the story as evidence for your statement.

5. How did Buck's life change again at Skaguay?

6. When Buck lay by the fire at night, did his thoughts of Judge Miller's place make him feel homesick? Explain why or why not.

7. Who was the man that Buck imagined seeing by the fire? Why would this be in Buck's memory or consciousness?

8. When Dave became ill after leaving Dawson, how did he show his "pride of trace"? What was his fate in the end?

Chapter Five: The Toil of Trace and Trail

1. What caused the Scotch half-breed to part from the team?

2. Hal is described as a callous or heartless man. What piece of equipment "advertised his callousness"?

3. How did Buck react when the sled tipped over in Skaguay?

4. The people of Skaguay give Hal, Charles and Mercedes some advice to help them on their way. What did they suggest they do?

5. How did the team feel about the situation they were in?

6. Hal, Charles and Mercedes had overlooked a vital necessity. What was it?

7. Describe the "wonderful patience of the trail" and the kind of people who demonstrated it.

8. How had Mercedes previous life affected her behavior on the trail?

9. London describes the "beautiful spring weather" in the Yukon and the awakening of nature as a background to the team's final misery. List two of the springtime scenes he refers to in this chapter.

10. Why was Thornton reluctant to offer advice to Hal?

11. Buck refused to get up and pull the sled at Thornton's camp. Why do you think he refused and was he right to do so?

The Call of the Wild

By Jack London

Chapter Six: For the Love of a Man

1. Compare Buck's relationship with Thornton with the one he had with Judge Miller. How are they different?

2. Do you think Buck's (civilized) emotions, such as love, overcame his wilder instincts when he was with Thornton? Explain why or why not. Support your answer with evidence from this chapter.

3. How did Buck physically express his love for Thornton?

4. Compare and contrast the way Thornton, Judge Miller, Francois, Perrault and the Scotch half-breed treated Buck. What did Thornton do that made him the "ideal master"?

5. Sometimes loving someone can cause a person to feel afraid of losing them. How did Buck demonstrate this fear?

6. Why couldn't mercy "exist in the primordial life"?

7. Who were "the shades" that beckoned to Buck?

8. Buck demonstrated his loyalty to Thornton several times in this chapter. Give two examples of how he did this.

Chapter Seven: The Sounding of the Call

1. What do you think London meant when he wrote "John Thornton asked little of man or nature"?

2. When did Buck realize that he was answering "the call"? Why did he hesitate and return to camp?

3. During Buck's hunts there is evidence that the Yeehats have returned. Identify the evidence you noticed in this chapter.

4. Why do you think the Yeehats killed Thornton, Hans and Pete? Remember this story happens in the late 1890's.

5. Do you think Buck was justified in his revenge? Explain why or why not.

6. When Buck killed the Yeehats he allowed passion to overcome reason and cunning. Think of a time when something happened to you that caused you to "lose your head" for a moment. Describe what it was and how you reacted.

7. What had caused the Yeehats to return to this valley?

8. Even though Buck is now living with a wolf pack and Thornton is dead, he does not forget his beloved master. How do we know this?

The Call of the Wild

By Jack London

Chapter Analysis Questions

(Teacher Copy)

Chapter One:

1. In the beginning of the story Jack London uses descriptive phrases to establish the scene at Judge Miller's place. List four descriptive phrases that he used. Example *wide-spreading lawns. (wide cool verandah, gravelled driveways, interlacing boughs of tall poplars, vine-clad servants' cottages, long grape arbours, green pastures, roaring library fire: pages 9, 10, 18, 19)*

2. Jack London creates an image of Buck as a king. Locate evidence of this image *on page 10 and 11 and record one description of Buck as King. ("And over this great demesne Buck ruled" p. 10; "The whole realm was his" p. 10; "Among terriers he stalked imperiously .. for he was king - king over all the creeping, crawling, flying things of Judge Miller's place, humans included" p. 10, 11; "in right royal fashion" p. 11; "life of a sated aristocrat" p. 11)*

3. *What breeds of dogs were Buck's mother and father? (father - St. Bernard, mother - Scotch Shepherd p. 11)*

4. Which phrase on page 12 best describes Buck's rage at being dognapped? *("never in his whole life had he been so angry")*

5. On page 14 London shows us Buck's point of view about the situation. Summarize *Buck's perspective on the plight he found himself in. (Buck did not understand what was happening to him, but he had a sense that tough times lay ahead)*

6. Buck is no longer the same dog. His experiences have changed him forever. *Describe the change that has come over Buck on page 15. (Buck has changed from the judge's loyal companion to a fighting ball of fury)*

7. *How is Buck introduced to "the reign of primitive law"? (He is clubbed by the dog-breaker: page 19)*

8. What does London mean when he writes that "a man with a club was a lawgiver, a master to be obeyed, though not necessarily conciliated" *(page 19)*? Why do you think it was necessary for London to portray Buck as a dog who would not *conciliate? (It was necessary to obey the commands of a man with a club, but Buck did not act submissive by licking the man's hand or wagging his tail, he kept his pride: page 19)*

The Call of the Wild

By Jack London

9. Perrault becomes Buck's new owner. What character traits or qualities did Perrault **possess that earned Buck's respect? (He was fair, calm, impartial in administering justice and wise in the ways of dogs: pages 20, 21)**

10. Identify three qualities of Buck's that you would have admired. Give reasons for your choices.

Chapter Two:

1. Why were there "neither peace, nor rest, nor a moment's safety for Buck on Dyea **Beach"? (Both men and dogs were a constant threat to Buck's life: page 23)**

2. **What lesson did Buck learn from the attack on Curly? (When in a fight, never go down or the others will finish you off: page 24)**

3. **Why did Buck develop a hatred for Spitz in this chapter? (Spitz found the death of Curly amusing: page 24)**

4. **Describe the wolf manner of fighting. (Strike and leap away, while the others form a circle around the combatants, waiting to finish off the loser: page 24)**

5. **How did Buck learn to survive the bitterly cold nights? (He accidentally fell into Billee's hole in the snow and learned to make his own each night: page 27)**

6. Notice the human qualities London gives Buck in this chapter. List three of these. **(sorrow for Curly's death, sense of fairness, bad dreams, humiliation at first at having to do physical labor)**

7. Identify the experience Buck has that drives him back to "the lives of his forebears" **on page 28. (the feeling of being trapped in his snow cave upon awakening)**

8. The sled dogs Sol-leks and Dave had two ambitions in life. What were they? **(to be left alone: page 26; to pull sleds well: page 29)**

9. Buck soon adapted to the "law of club and fang". Describe the event in this **chapter that demonstrated Buck was fit to survive a harsh environment. (the theft of bacon from Perrault: page 31)**

10. Why would respecting personal feelings and property and other civilized behavior **be a handicap in the North? (It was essential to take opportunities when they came, such as food, and use primitive cunning to defend oneself. A "civilized" dog, example: Curly, would not survive: page 32)**

The Call of the Wild

By Jack London

11. London describes Buck's "internal and external economy" on page 33. Explain what he means by this phrase. *(Buck could eat anything, his body used every nutrient to its fullest, he developed an acute sense of sight and scent, and the ability to predict wind direction)*

12. London refers to life as a "puppet thing" on page 34. What do you think he means by this, in terms of Buck's response to the call of the wild?

Chapter Three:

1. Which event finally triggered Buck's attack on Spitz and what postponed the duel? *(Spitz stole Buck's sleeping hole; the attack by the starving huskies: page 36, 37)*

2. What dangers did the team face crossing the Thirty Mile River and how was Perrault saved? *(thin ice, frost bite, hypothermia; his long pole: page 39)*

3. What caused Dolly to "go mad" on page 42? *(she had been bitten by a husky with rabies)*

4. London uses conversations between Francois and Perrault to provide commentary on Buck's character and to predict possible future events. Do you think London's use of phonetic spelling to convey their accent is effective? Give reasons for your statement.

5. Spitz felt his leadership was threatened by Buck. What kind of primitive character traits had Buck developed that posed a threat to Spitz? *(strength, savagery, cunning and patience: page 43)*

6. How did the "pride of toil and trace" transform Dave and Sol-leks? *(they became straining, eager, ambitious and proud sled dogs: page 43)*

7. Buck likes to interfere when Spitz has arguments with other dogs. Why do you think London refers to this as "covert mutiny" and what is the effect on the team? *(Buck always acted when Francois was not around and encouraged the other dogs to rebel, rather than openly doing so himself: page 44; the dogs became less afraid of Spitz, they quarreled with each other instead of maintaining solidarity pages 44-46)*

8. On page 48 London describes "an ecstasy that marks the summit of life, and beyond which life cannot rise ... this ecstasy comes when one is most alive, and it comes as a complete forgetfulness that one is alive." This is a time when we are so caught up in the joy of what we are doing, that we are oblivious of all else. Brainstorm and suggest a moment when someone could experience "this forgetfulness of living" other than what is given in the text.

The Call of the Wild

By Jack London

9. At the beginning of Buck's fight with Spitz, the scene of the battle became somehow familiar to Buck? How could this happen? *(the collective memories of the primitive lives of his ancestors were within Buck)*

10. What characteristics of a "practised fighter" did Spitz demonstrate? *(he never attacked until he had defended his opponents rush, was very calculating: page 50)*

11. "Buck possessed a quality that made for greatness (page 51). What was this quality and how did he use it to win the fight with Spitz and become the "dominant primordial beast"? *(imagination; Buck faked "the old shoulder trick" and at the last moment he swept low and in on Spitz's legs, breaking each of his front legs: page 51)*

Chapter Four:

1. How does Francois describe Buck? Why? *(two devils - his defeat of Spitz and worth $1,000 because of his value as lead dog: page 53, 57)*

2. How does Buck react when Francois places Sol-leks in the lead dog position? Explain his reasons for behaving this way. *(Buck attacks Sol-leks and drives him away and takes the lead dog position himself; he believes it is his right now he has defeated Spitz: page 52, 53)*

3. Think about the part of the story where London writes "Buck laughed, as dogs laugh.." How might a dog laugh? What kind of body language would they use to demonstrate their amusement? *(tongue hanging out, eyes bright: page 55)*

4. Decide if Buck's leadership had a positive or negative effect on the team? Give an example from the story as evidence for your statement. *(Buck's leadership had a positive effect on the team; they recovered their old team solidarity as Buck enforced discipline: pages 55, 56)*

5. How did Buck's life change again at Skaguay? *(he was sold to a Scotch half-breed to pull sleds on the mail train: page 58)*

6. When Buck lay by the fire at night, did his thoughts of Judge Miller's place make him feel homesick? Explain why or why not. *(He was not homesick, these memories were not important to him now, his recent experiences and the return of his animal instincts were more relevant: page 61)*

7. Who was the man that Buck imagined seeing by the fire? Why would this be in Buck's memory or consciousness? *(a prehistoric man: this memory was triggered by Buck's retrogression to a wild state, a life driven by instinct: page 60)*

The Call of the Wild

By Jack London

8. When Dave became ill after leaving Dawson, how did he show his "pride of trace"? What was his fate in the end? **(he tried to get back in his old position by rushing at Sol-leks and refusing to follow behind the sled; he bit through Sol-leks traces and stood in his old position; the Scotch half-breed shoots him to end his suffering: pages 62-64)**

Chapter Five:

1. What caused the Scotch half-breed to part from the team? **(he received orders to sell Buck's team and take fresh Hudson Bay dogs: page 66)**

2. Hal is described as a callous or heartless man. What piece of equipment "advertised his callousness"? **(his belt full of revolver cartridges: page 67)**

3. How did Buck react when the sled tipped over in Skaguay? **(he led the team in a fast run up the street: page 72)**

4. The people of Skaguay give Hal, Charles and Mercedes some advice to help them on their way. What did they suggest they do? **(cut the load in half and get more sled dogs: page 72)**

5. How did the team feel about the situation they were in? **(the old team dogs had no confidence in their new masters; the new ones were frightened: page 74)**

6. Hal, Charles and Mercedes had overlooked a vital necessity. What was it? **(a sled could not carry enough food for fourteen dogs and they were sure to starve: page 74)**

7. Describe the "wonderful patience of the trail" and the kind of people who demonstrated it. **(to remain kind and good natured during harsh conditions; people who work hard and suffer long: page 76)**

8. How had Mercedes previous life affected her behavior on the trail? **(she was used to being treated as a lady and now she was expected to ride on the sled and do a little work: page 77)**

9. London describes the "beautiful spring weather" in the Yukon and the awakening of nature as a background to the team's final misery. List two of the springtime scenes he refers to in this chapter. **(the new growth on the shrubs and vines, sap rising in the pines, the buds on the willows and aspens, crickets singing at night, partridges and woodpeckers in the forest, squirrels chattering, birds singing, trickling water in the rivers: page 80)**

10. Why was Thornton reluctant to offer advice to Hal? **(he knew that it would not be followed: page 81)**

The
Call of the Wild

By Jack London

11. Buck refused to get up and pull the sled at Thornton's camp. Why do you think he **refused and was he right to do so? (he had a feeling that something was going to happen on the soft ice; he was right to do so, as the team did fall through the ice and drown: page 82)**

Chapter Six:

1. Compare Buck's relationship with Thornton with the one he had with Judge Miller. **How are they different? (Buck adores Thornton with a passion, while his relationship with the judge was a "dignified friendship": page 86)**

2. Do you think Buck's (civilized) emotions, such as love, overcame his wilder instincts when he was with Thornton? Explain why or why not. Support your answer with evidence from this chapter.

3. **How did Buck physically express his love for Thornton? (he would seize Thornton's hand in his mouth in a playful bite: page 87)**

4. Compare and contrast the way Thornton, Judge Miller, Francois, Perrault and the Scotch half-breed treated Buck. What did Thornton do that made him the "ideal **master"? (he looked after his dogs as if they were his own children, talked to them and played with them: page 86-87)**

5. Sometimes loving someone can cause a person to feel afraid of losing them. How **did Buck demonstrate this fear? (he would creep up to Thornton's tent at night to check if he was still there: page 88)**

6. **Why couldn't mercy "exist in the primordial life"? (it was interpreted as fear and weakness, which was fatal; kill or be killed was the law: page 89)**

7. **Who were "the shades" that beckoned to Buck? (his wild ancestors and the wolves that lived in the forest surrounding him: page 89)**

8. Buck demonstrated his loyalty to Thornton several times in this chapter. Give two **examples of how he did this. (when Thornton commanded him to jump over the edge of a cliff, Buck obeyed and began to jump; he attacked a man in Circle City who had hit Thornton; he rescued Thornton from the rapids; he pulled a sled with a 1,000 pound load a hundred yards: pages 91, 93-95)**

The Call of the Wild

By Jack London

Chapter Seven:

1. What do you think London meant when he wrote "John Thornton asked little of man *or nature"? (he could survive in the wild with just a rifle and a handful of salt: page 104)*

2. When did Buck realize that he was answering "the call"? Why did he hesitate and *return to camp? (when he was running alongside the timber wolf; he remembered Thornton: page 109)*

3. During Buck's hunts there is evidence that the Yeehats have returned. Identify the *evidence you noticed in this chapter. (there is a feathered arrow protruding from the moose's flank: page 114)*

4. Why do you think the Yeehats killed Thornton, Hans and Pete? Remember this story happens in the late 1890's.

5. Do you think Buck was justified in his revenge? Explain why or why not.

6. When Buck killed the Yeehats he allowed passion to overcome reason and cunning. Think of a time when something happened to you that caused you to "lose your head" for a moment. Describe what it was and how you reacted.

7. *What had caused the Yeehats to return to this valley? (the moose were migrating in the fall, and they followed them there: page 121)*

8. Even though Buck is now living with a wolf pack and Thornton is dead, he does not *forget his beloved master. How do we know this? (Buck returns to the campsite in the valley each summer and howls in sadness: page 124)*

The Call of the Wild

By Jack London

Character Activity #1

Character Comparison

In the novel Buck overcomes a number of tests or hardships.

Did the ways in which Buck overcame these obstacles remind you of a character in another story?

What character traits enabled them to succeed?

List the titles of **three** novels, the name of the character in each and describe the tests or obstacles they overcame in the chart below.

Novel	Character	Test or Obstacle

The
Call of the Wild

By Jack London

Character Activity #2

Buck the Hero

Buck demonstrates many of the personal qualities or character traits of a hero.

Support this statement with the evidence from the story.

Present your evidence in the form of a chart.

Example:

Character Traits of a Hero	Evidence Buck is a Hero
intelligent	
strong	
wise	
brave	

The
Call of the Wild

By Jack London

Character Activity #3

Character Web

London created Buck as a powerful character in the novel. He was able to do this by describing his:

- **feelings**
- **behavior**
- **physical appearance**
- **personality traits**

List examples of how London described each of these in a web.

Example:

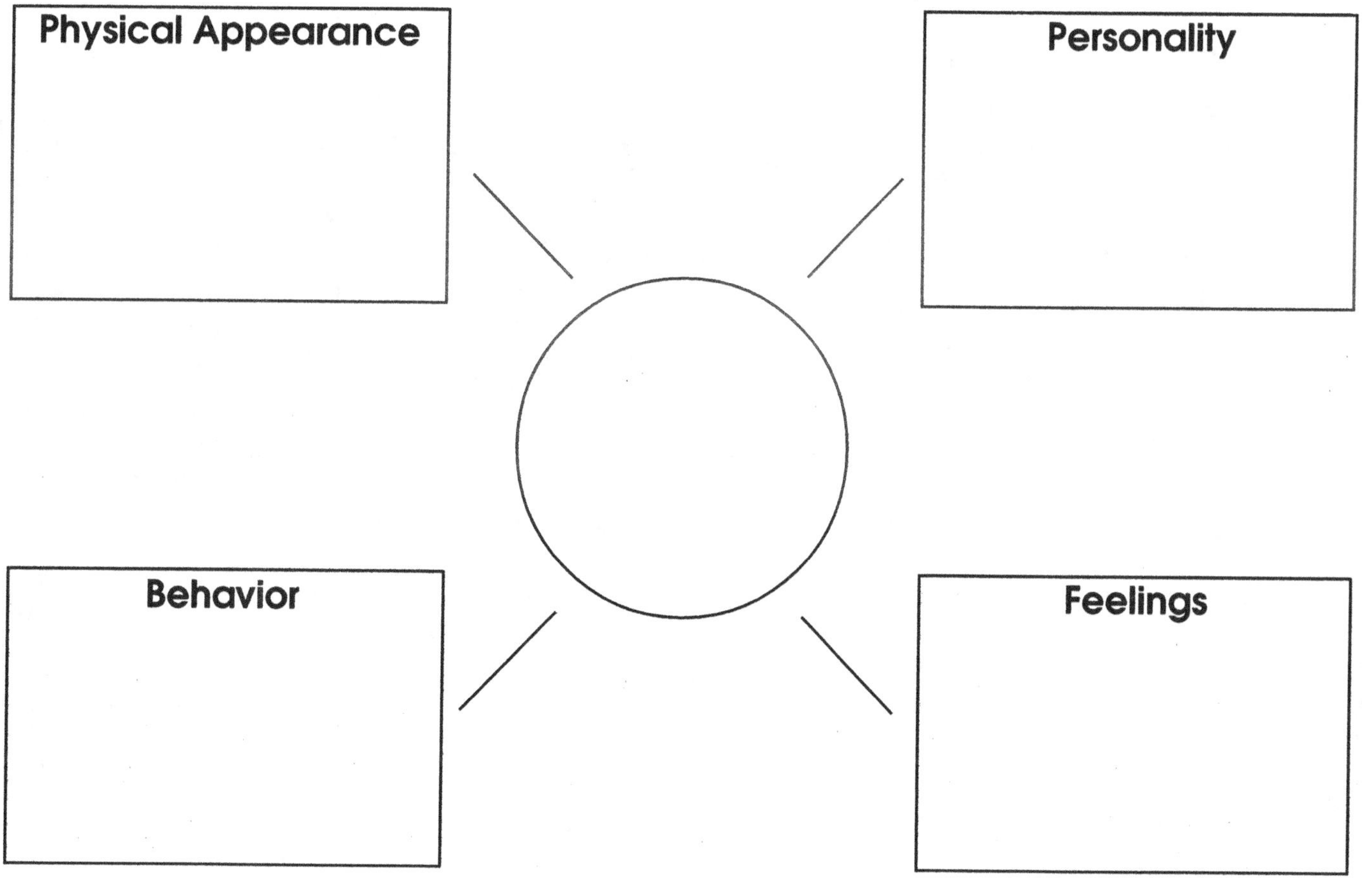

Physical Appearance

Personality

Behavior

Feelings

The Call of the Wild

By Jack London

Character Activity #4

Literary Sociogram

A literary sociogram is a diagram that represents the interrelationships between characters in a novel.

Each relationship has a two way effect.

Label each arrow with a word or phrase that describes how that character felt towards the other.

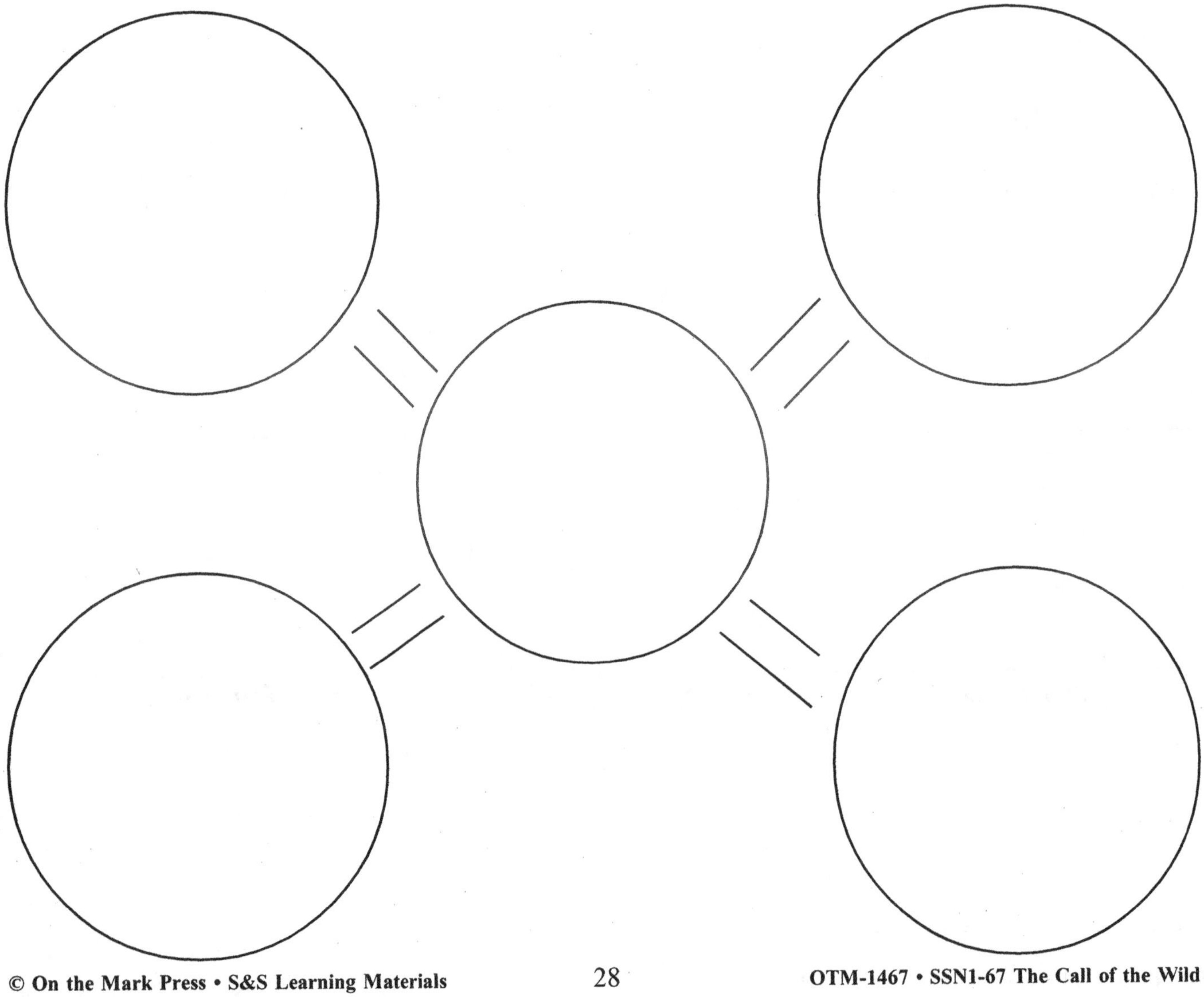

The Call of the Wild

By Jack London

Character Activity #5

Who Said It?

In the "Call of the Wild", Jack London uses conversation between characters to give the reader an understanding of the characters.

Read the statements below. Match each statement to the character who said it.

Characters

John Thornton	**Perrault**
Francois	**Man in red sweater**
Mercedes	**Pete**
Hal	

---

1. "Now, you red-eyed devil." _____

2. "Dat Buck for sure learn queek as anyt'ing." _____

3. "You poor, poor dears." _____

4. "Dat Buck two devils." _____

5. "The lazy brutes, I'll show them." _____

6. "I wouldn't risk my carcass on that ice for all_____
   the gold in Alaska."

7. "I'm not hankering to be the man that lays_____
   hands on you while he's around."

8. "God, you can all but speak." _____

The
Call of the Wild

By Jack London

Character Activity #6

Character Role

Every character has a role to play.

Think about the roles each of the characters in "Call of the Wild" had to play.

Match the roles below to the list of characters in the novel.

> ### Character Roles
>
> **hero**   **fool**   **companion**
>
> **victim**   **villain**

1. Buck   _____

2. man in red sweater   _____

3. Thornton   _____

4. Hal   _____

5. Curly   _____

Illustrate each character's face in the box below.

The Call of the Wild

By Jack London

Character Activity #7

Picture Paragraphs

Each character in "Call of the Wild" had a role to play and a particular type of personality.

Read the list of characters in the story.

Draw a picture of each one.

Beside each picture write a summary explaining the part they played in the story.

Buck
Hal
Thornton
Perrault
Man in the red sweater

The Call of the Wild

By Jack London

Character Activity #8

Man or Beast?

When an author gives human characteristics and personality traits to an animal we call it personification. The author is describing their actions and feelings as if they were a person.

Jack London used personification to portray Buck as a strong and sympathetic character.

Think about the ways Buck is like a real person.

List at least four human characteristics he demonstrated.

Describe how Buck demonstrated each one using examples from the story.

Example:

Human Characteristic	Example
anger	Buck is angry when he is dognapped
love	Buck loves Thornton with a passion

The
Call of the Wild

By Jack London

Character Activity #9

Flat and Round Characters

A flat character is one that does not grow or change in the story.

A round character changes and grows in the story.

Choose a flat and round character in the novel "Call of the Wild".

Describe each character and explain why they are round or flat characters.

Example:

Hal is cruel and arrogant in the novel. He does not listen to the advice the townspeople or Thornton give him about the needs of dogs or the danger of traveling on thin ice. Hal only thinks of himself and continues in his ignorance until his end. This makes him a flat character in the novel.

Round Character: _____

_____

_____

_____

_____

_____

_____

Flat Character: _____

_____

_____

_____

_____

_____

The
Call of the Wild

By Jack London

Character Activity #10

Character Comparison

There are many different adventure stories with a dog as the central character.

Compare Buck's character to a dog character in another book you have read. <u>Example:</u> "Old Yeller", "White Fang", "Big Red" or "Tuck".

Create a chart comparing the two characters.

How are they alike?

How are they different?

Example:

Characteristic	Buck	Old Yeller
loyal		
brave		
intelligent		
physical strength		
wild		
independent		
leader		
fighter		

The Call of the Wild

By Jack London

Setting Activity #1

Novel Scenes

The setting of a novel describes where and when the story takes place.

Think of different settings that Jack London describes in the novel "The Call of the Wild".

List three settings and give details from the novel describing each one.

Example:

1. Setting: Judge Miller's place in Santa Clara Valley, California

    Details: a wide, cool verandah, gravelled driveways, long grape arbors, green pastures, roaring library fire, vine-clad servants' cottages

2. Setting: _____

    _____

    Details: _____

    _____

    _____

3. Setting: _____

    _____

    Details _____

    _____

4. Setting: _____

    _____

    Details: _____

    _____

    _____

The
Call of the Wild

By Jack London

Jack London illustrates many of the dangers experienced by people and dogs during the Klondike Gold Rush.

List the dangers and survival tips referred to in the novel.

Use a chart to present your novel research.

Example:

Compare	Dangers	Survival Tips
Dogs		
People		

The
Call of the Wild

By Jack London

Setting #4

Mapping the Route

Buck began his life in Santa Clara Valley, California. His new life began when he was dognapped and taken as a sled dog to the Yukon.

Use an atlas to trace the route Buck followed in his adventures.

You will need to locate:

1. **Santa Clara Valley, California**

2. **San Francisco**

3. **Dyea Beach**

4. **Skaguay (Skaguay)**

5. **Dawson City**

6. **Circle City**

Label the blank map with each location.

Join them together with a colored line.

Look at the scale on your map.

How far is it from San Francisco to Skaguay? _____

The Call of the Wild

By Jack London

Setting Activity #5

Time Capsule

The novel "Call of the Wild" belongs to the genre of book called historical fiction.

This means it is an imaginary story based on historical events.

A time capsule contains information about and objects from a specific historic period.

The story of Buck's life in "Call of the Wild" began in 1897.

Think about the types of information and objects a time capsule from this time period would contain.

Research in reference books such as encyclopedias to find our about life in the 1890's.

Draw a time capsule containing objects from this time.

List the items it contains.

Example:

My time Capsule contains:

_____

_____

_____

_____

_____

_____

_____

The Call of the Wild

By Jack London

Setting Activity #6

Story Map

The setting in the novel changes from Buck's first home in Santa Clara Valley to his new life in the Yukon.

List four of the main settings for this novel.

Sequence them in order that they appeared in the story.

Illustrate the settings in the form of a story map.

Think about how they were described. How will you represent them in a visual form?

Create a colorful map.

You will need to include:

- symbols and pictures
- titles and labels for places and objects in the setting
- a legend for your map

Example:

```
┌──────────────────┐        ┌──────────────────┐
│                  │   ←    │                  │
│                  │        │                  │
└────────┬─────────┘        └──────────────────┘
         │                            ↑
         ↓                            │
┌──────────────────┐        ┌──────────────────┐
│                  │   →    │                  │
│                  │        │                  │
└──────────────────┘        └──────────────────┘
```

The Call of the Wild

By Jack London

Plot Activity #1

Graphing the Plot

In "The Call of the Wild" Jack London created exciting events throughout the story to keep our interest.

Identify ten of the main events of the story.

Order them in sequence.

Think about the level of intensity or excitement you felt when you read each event.

Draw a bar graph to show the level of intensity of each of these events.

Write a short description of the event inside each bar of your graph.

Label the left side of your graph "Intensity Scale".

Label the bottom of your graph "Story Events".

The Call of the Wild

By Jack London

Plot Activity #2

A Different Ending

The novel "The Call of the Wild" ends with the death of John Thornton and Buck's return to the life of his wild ancestors.

How else could this story have ended?

Think about how you might have changed this last chapter.

Write your own concluding chapter to "The Call of the Wild".

You will need to include at least three paragraphs.

The Call of the Wild

By Jack London

Plot Activity #3

Cloze It!

A cloze activity has important words or phrases that are missing.

Summarize the main events in "Call of the Wild".

Complete each sentence starter with information from the story.

First Buck, _____

_____

_____

_____

This _____

_____

_____

_____

As a result _____

_____

_____

_____

Then _____

_____

_____

_____

In the end _____

_____

_____

_____

This is the reason _____

_____

_____

_____

The Call of the Wild

By Jack London

Plot Activity #4

Resolving Story Problems

Think about the problem Buck faced in this story.

What was his main goal or motivation?

What important events lead to Buck achieving this goal?

How was his problem finally resolved?

Complete your answers to these questions in the form of a flow chart.

Example:

Problem

Goal

Event #1	Event #2	Event #3

Resolution

The Call of the Wild

By Jack London

Plot Activity #5

Cause and Effect

The Klondike Gold Rush changed the lives of the characters in this novel for ever.

Many incidents were caused by this one event.

Complete a diagram like the one below illustrating how the Klondike Gold Rush affected each character.

List **one** event caused by the Gold Rush in each circle.

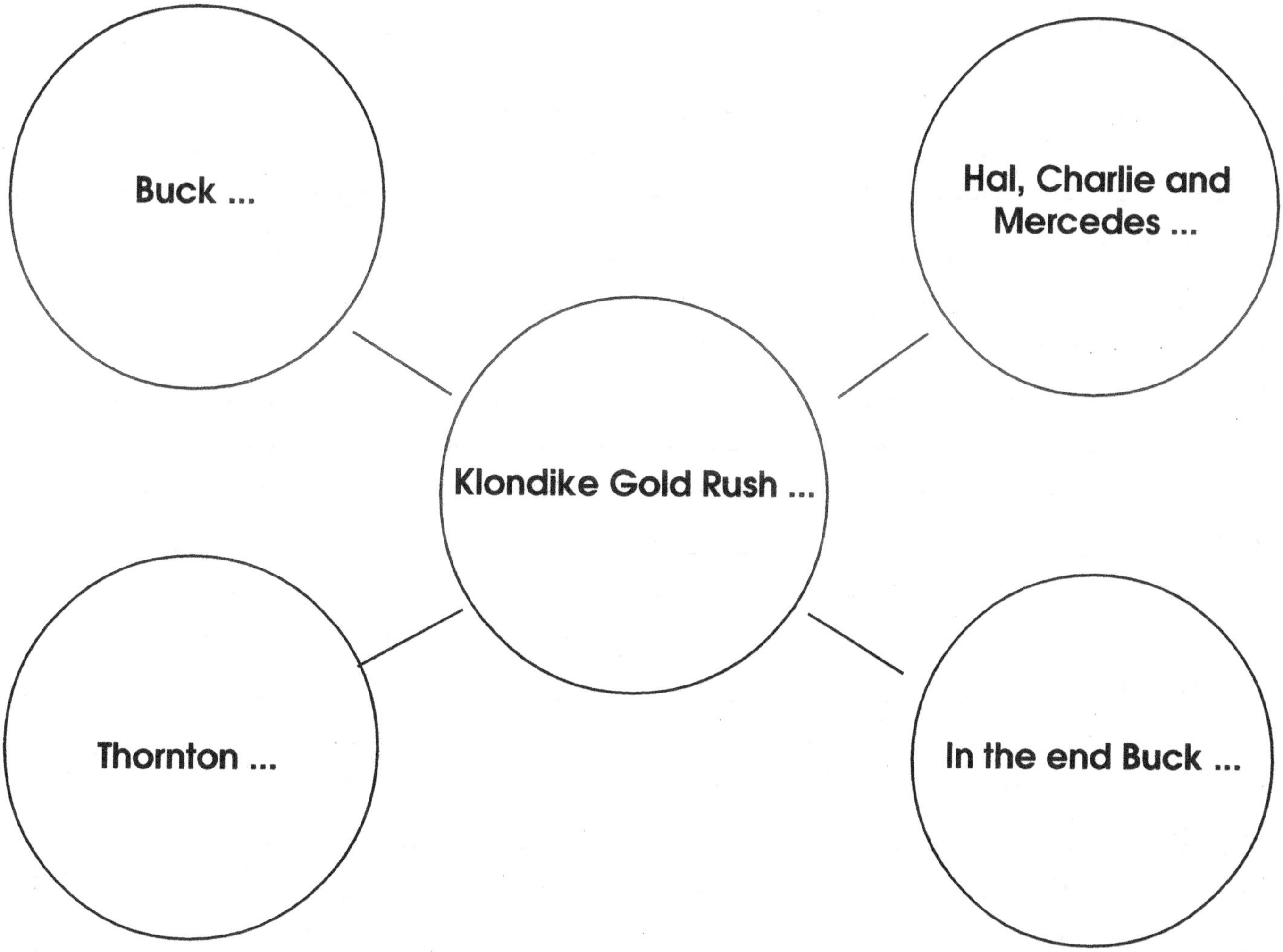

Buck ...

Hal, Charlie and Mercedes ...

Klondike Gold Rush ...

Thornton ...

In the end Buck ...

The Call of the Wild

By Jack London

Plot Activity #6

Story Grammar

An author must create a plot or framework to build their story.

This includes:

- theme (central message or main idea of the story)
- setting (time and place)
- characters
- problem or conflict
- climax (peak of conflict, just before the problem is solved)
- ending

Summarize each element of the plot in "Call of the Wild".

Complete the story grammar below.

Setting: _____

_____

_____

Characters: _____

_____

_____

Problem or Conflict: _____

_____

_____

Climax: _____

_____

_____

Resolution: _____

_____

_____

Ending: _____

_____

_____

The Call of the Wild

By Jack London

Plot Activity #7

Story Countdown

Think about the most important events in the story.

What happened at the beginning of the story?

What happened at the end?

List **ten** main events in point form.

Sequence these events in the order that they happened.

Number each event in the form of a countdown.

Number 10 will describe an event at the beginning of the story.

Number 1 will describe an event at the end of the story.

Example:

10. Buck lived with Judge Miller in Santa Clara Valley.
9. _____
8. _____
7. _____
6. _____
5. _____
4. _____
3. _____
2. _____
1. Buck joined the wolves in the forest to live as his wild ancestors had once lived.

The Call of the Wild

By Jack London

Plot Activity #8

Conflict in the Story

In the novel "Call of the Wild" we follow the conflicts Buck faces in his new life and learn how he resolves each one.

Authors may use four types of conflict in a novel. They are:

1. *character against character*
2. *character against nature*
3. *character against society*
4. *character against him/herself*

Choose **one** of the four types of conflict illustrated in the novel.

Explain why this conflict occurs and how it is solved using the information in the story.

Write your answer in a paragraph.

Your paragraph will need to include:

- *a statement telling the reader what the conflict was about in the story and what type of conflict it is*

- *at least three points why the conflict occurred and how it is solved*

- *a conclusion summing up this conflict*

The
Call of the Wild

By Jack London

Creative and Critical Thinking Activity #1

Natural Resources

The people who lived in the Yukon during the Klondike Gold Rush had to learn how to use nature's resources to survive.

Research in reference books for information on the natural resources of the Yukon.

Make a chart of the natural resources available to them in the Yukon. Describe how each one was used at the time of the story.

Example:

Natural Resources	People's Use

The
Call of the Wild

By Jack London

Creative and Critical Thinking Activity #2

Novel Substitutions

An author has to make a number of decisions as he writes a novel.

These decisions create the plot as we read it.

But what if:

1. *One of the characters had not been in the story?*

2. *One of the characters did something different?*

3. *Something had not happened at all?*

How would one of these have changed the story?

For example, what would have happened in "Call of the Wild" if:

- **Hal, Charles and Mercedes had not bought Buck?**

- **Thornton had not been killed?**

- **Buck had not joined the wolves in the forest after Thornton's death?**

- **Buck had not been able to pull the 1,000 pound sled and Thornton did not have the money to search for the lost mine? What other adventures might they have had?**

Write a brief summary of the novel the way you think it could have been if one of these had happened.

The
Call of the Wild

By Jack London

Creative and Critical Thinking Activity #3

Letter Form the North

Imagine you are living in the Yukon.

It is the year 1897.

Decide if you are a gold miner, mail train sled driver, shopkeeper or a policeman?

What stories could you tell the folks back home?

Write a letter home describing your adventures in the northland.

The
Call of the Wild

By Jack London

Creative and Critical Thinking Activity #4

Inventors and Their Inventions

"Buck possessed a quality that made for greatness - imagination." (page 51)

Many men and women have also possessed this quality and used it to attain greatness in both the past and present.

Brainstorm and list two inventors whose imaginations led to a great discovery.

List their names and describe what they invented.

You may wish to research in reference books for specific details.

The Call of the Wild

By Jack London

Creative and Critical Thinking Activity #5

Survival of the Fittest

Buck possessed certain personality traits that determined his chance of survival.

Review the characters listed in the chart.

Describe the qualities each one possessed that enabled them to survive.

Characters	Traits That Enabled Them to Survive
Spitz	**e.g.** tough, experienced fighter, pride in his work
Thornton	**e.g.** able to survive with a rifle and a handful of salt
Buck	
Perrault	
Sol-leks	

The Call of the Wild

By Jack London

Creative and Critical Thinking Activity #6

Cruelty Against Animals

Imagine that charges have been brought against the man in the red sweater for his abuse of Buck.

List the charges that would be brought against him under the heading "Accusations" and the evidence supporting each accusation.

Describe how he would argue to defend himself under the heading "Defense".

List the evidence he could use.

Decide if the jury would find him guilty or not guilty. If they find him guilty, what will be his punishment?

Example:

Accusations:	Defense:
1. _____	1. _____
2. _____	2. _____
3. _____	3. _____

Evidence:	Evidence:
_____	_____
_____	_____
_____	_____

Jury's Decision:

_____

_____

_____

The
Call of the Wild

By Jack London

Creative and Critical Thinking Activity #7

Wild, Domesticated or Both?

At times, Buck demonstrated qualities of a dog that is domesticated, such as loyalty to a master.

At other times he behaved like a wild wolf, fighting to the death and hunting for his food.

Brainstorm and list qualities of both domesticated dogs and wolves.

How are they alike? How are they different?

Use a Venn diagram to show how they are different and how they are alike.

You may wish to use reference materials to locate information on wolves.

Example:

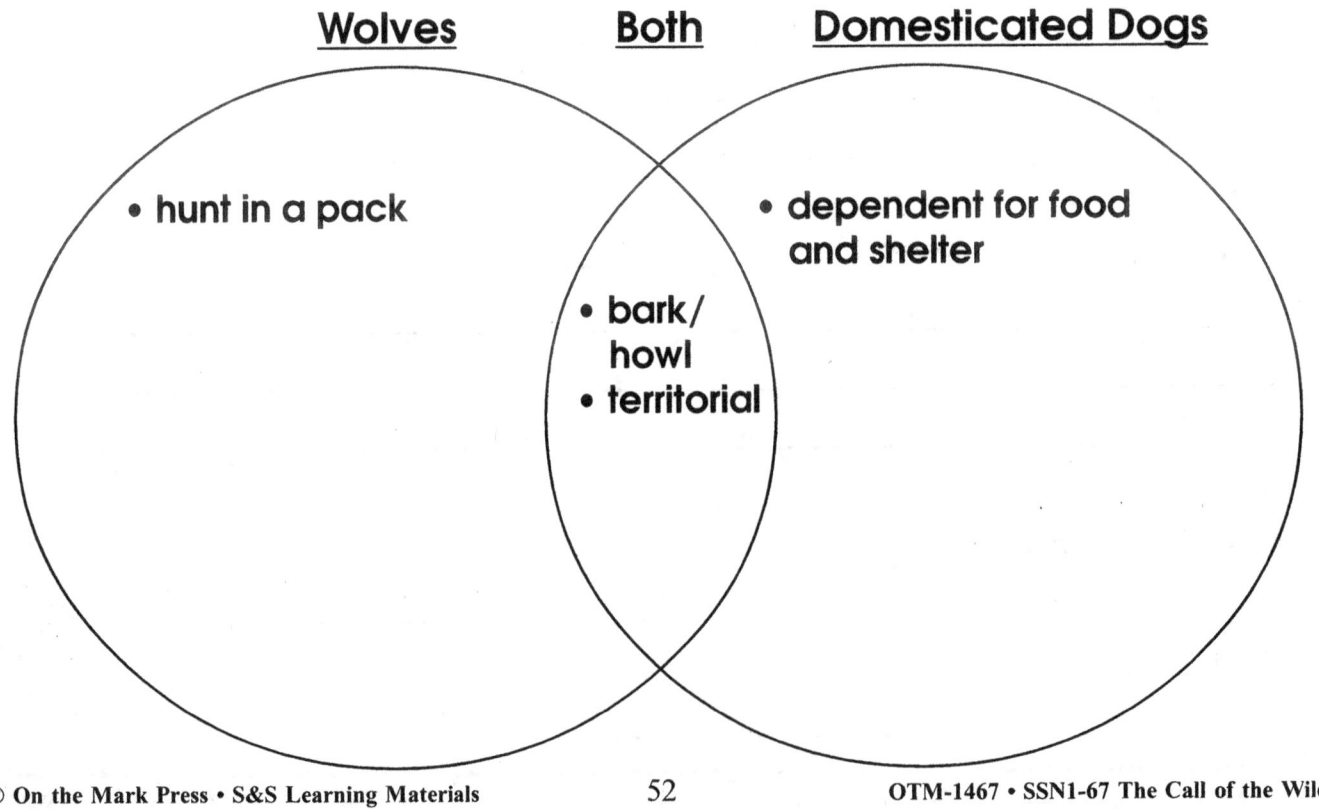

Wolves   **Both**   **Domesticated Dogs**

- hunt in a pack

- bark/ howl
- territorial

- dependent for food and shelter

The Call of the Wild

By Jack London

Creative and Critical Thinking Activity #8

Instincts and Emotions

In the novel Buck's animal instincts enabled him to survive in a very harsh environment.

Jack London describes how Buck feels drawn to the life of his wild ancestors; a life lived by instincts.

London also describes the emotions both Buck and the human characters in the story feel.

List the instincts Buck demonstrates and the emotions both he and the human characters display in the novel.

Write a paragraph on one instinct or emotion.

Explain how this was a benefit or a problem to the character. Use examples from the text to support your answer.

Example:

Buck's Instincts	Emotions of Buck and Human Characters
defend food and shelter	Buck's anger towards Spitz for being amused at Curly's death

Example Paragraph:

Buck demonstrated the instinct...
This first came to Buck when he...
It made it possible for him to ....
Buck was now ....
Such an instinct enabled him to withstand the very harsh winter conditions in the Yukon.

The Call of the Wild

By Jack London

Creative and Critical Thinking Activity #9

News Story

Summarize the story of Buck in a news report.

Look at the front page of a newspaper and read some of the articles.

What do you notice about the structure of a news article?

A news article should include:

1. **Headline:** tells what the story is about

2. **Dateline**: tells where the story came from and when it was written

3. **Slugline**: first sentence, tells what happened with a few details

4. **Body**: answers the questions Who? What? Where? When? Why? and How? It may include an interview with someone who witnessed the event.

Use this structure to create a news story based on the life of Buck.

You may wish to choose one particular event such as the sled pull in Circle City.

Think of a catchy headline to grab the reader's attention.

Example:

"Amazing Sled Dog Pulls 1,000 Pounds!"

or

"California Dog Becomes a Legend"

Will you include an interview with **one** of the characters or a bystander? What might they say about Buck?

The Call of the Wild

By Jack London

Vocabulary Development Activity #1

Definitions

Match each vocabulary word from the novel with its meaning.

Write the letter of the correct definition next to the word.

1. conciliated _____
2. progeny _____
3. primordial _____
4. retrogression _____
5. vicarious _____
6. precipitate _____
7. coveted _____
8. covert _____
9. callous _____
10. salient _____
11. superfluous _____
12. voracious _____
13. infinitesimal _____

a) unfeeling, hardhearted

b) prominent, easily seen, projecting

c) secret or hidden

d) pacified or soothed

e) to go backward to a former state

f) descendants, offspring

g) existing from the beginning, original

h) delegated to or performed by another

l) hasty and rash

j) desired or craved

k) a very small quantity

l) more than necessary

m) greedy for eating

The Call of the Wild

By Jack London

Vocabulary Development Activity #2

Similes or Metaphors

A simile compares two unlike things using the word "**like**" or "**as**".

> <u>Example:</u> " ... **dragging them down like deer ...**" (**page 119**)

A metaphor compares two unlike things suggesting that they are similar without using the word "like" or "as".

> <u>Example:</u> "**It was Buck, a live hurricane of fury ...**" (**page 118**)

Read each of the comparisons that were used in "Call of the Wild".

Decide if each one is a **metaphor** or a **simile** and write this next to the comparison.

1. His muscles were surcharged with vitality, and snapped into play sharply, like steel springs. _____

2. Like giants they toiled, days flashing on the heels of days like dreams as they heaped the treasure up. _____

3. Into the clearing, where the moonlight streamed, they poured in a silvery flood. _____

4. At the end of their wandering they found, not the Lost Cabin, but a shallow placer in a broad valley where the gold showed like yellow butter across the bottom of the washing pan.

    _____

5. ...and in the centre of the clearing stood Buck, motionless as a statue, waiting for their coming. _____

6. A carnivorous animal, living on a straight meat diet, he was in full flower, at the high tide of his life, overspilling with vigor and virility.

    _____

The Call of the Wild

By Jack London

Vocabulary Development Activity #3

Descriptive Words and Phrases

An author uses descriptive words and phrases to help the reader understand something about a character or a setting in the novel.

For example Jack London describes Buck's new home in the Yukon as a "hostile Northland environment." (page 32)

Locate **six** additional descriptive words or phrases in the novel and note the page number you found it on.

Identify the object, scene or character London is describing. Record this next to its description in the form of a chart.

Example:

Subject	Description
Buck	a carnivorous animal (page 112)

The
Call of the Wild

By Jack London

Vocabulary Development Activity #4

Opposites

An antonym is a word that means the opposite.

Read the list of words from the novel below.

List the **opposite** or **antonym** of each word.

1. cruel   _____

2. conspicuous   _____

3. honest   _____

4. powerful   _____

5. gentle   _____

6. stubborn   _____

7. dominant   _____

8. generous   _____

9. ecstasy   _____

10. foolish   _____

11. suspicious   _____

12. trusting   _____

13. imaginative   _____

14. necessary   _____

The Call of the Wild

By Jack London

Vocabulary Development Activity #5

Synonyms

A synonym is a word that means the same or has a similar meaning.

Create a list of synonyms for each word in the chart.

List at least **two** synonyms for each word.

toil	intelligent	wild

cruel	call	law

The
Call of the Wild

By Jack London

Vocabulary Development Activity #6

Context Clues

Choose a word from the vocabulary list to complete each sentence.

Write the correct word in the space.

Vocabulary List				
progeny	*revelation*	*primitive*	*pandemonium*	*paradox*
score	*covert*	*squabbling*	*primordial*	

1. For to pay, a system requires money, while the wages of a gardener's helper do not cover the needs of a wife and numerous

   _____.

2. He had learned a lesson, and in all his after life he never forgot it. The club was a _____.

3. He was pre-eminently cunning, and could bide his time with a patience that was nothing less than _____.

4. An oath from Perrault, the resounding impact of a club upon a bony frame, and a shrill yelp of pain, heralded the breaking forth of

   _____.

5. Dave and Sol-leks dripping blood from a _____ of wounds, were fighting side by side.

6. With the _____ mutiny of Buck a general insubordination sprang up and increased.

7. Dave and Sol-leks alone were unaltered, though they were made irritable by the unending _____.

8. Guided by instinct which came from the old hunting days of the _____ world, Buck proceeded to cut the bull from the herd.

9. And such is the _____ of living, the ecstasy comes when one is most alive, and it comes as a complete forgetfulness that one is alive.

The *Call of the Wild*

By Jack London

Art Activity #1

Travel Brochure

The Yukon is a place of great natural beauty. Capture this beauty in a travel brochure.

Fold a piece of 8 1/2" by 11" (14 cm by 27.5 cm) paper into three to make a three fold brochure.

You will need to include:

- **a cover page with a picture of the Yukon**

- **a description of places to see and special events such as sled dog races**

- **a list of places to stay such as campgrounds, motels and hotels**

The *Call of the Wild*

By Jack London

Art Activity #2

Illustrate a Scene

Jack London used vivid descriptions to illustrate the different scenes in his novel.

Think about one of the scenes in the novel. Draw a picture to recreate the scene.

What details will you need to include?

What objects were described in the text?

Would conversation bubbles or a thinking balloon help to represent what happened in that scene?

The Call of the Wild

By Jack London

Art Activity #3

Portrait of a Hero

On page 111 and 112 London describes Buck's heritage and physical appearance. What image does this create in your mind?

Draw a picture of Buck as you imagined him to be.

Think about what kind of expression he will have.

Which background scene will you use?

How will you create an image of an animal that is capable of both savageness and gentleness?

The Call of the Wild

By Jack London

Art Activity #4

Aurora Borealis

Create an Aurora Borealis.

Sprinkle a small amount of different powdered paints on a sheet of white paper.

Use a wet paint brush to blend them together into a swirl of color.

Let your paper dry completely.

Cut out a silhouette shape of black construction paper and glue them against the colored background.

Choose shapes that represent the north, such as a wolf, caribou, mountain, kayak or canoe.

The Call of the Wild

By Jack London

Art Activity #5

Cruelty to Animals Poster

Buck was treated cruelly by some of the humans in the story.

Design a poster to encourage people to prevent such cruelty to animals.

You will need to point out how they can help prevent such cruelty from continuing.

You may wish to use a logo for your poster.

The Call of the Wild

By Jack London

Art Activity #6

Missing Dog Poster

Re-read the description of Buck on page 111. Create a "missing persons" poster of Buck.

Use the description to draw a picture of Buck. You will also need to include the following facts about Buck under your drawing.

Name	**Weight**
Physical Description	**Special Features**
Fur Color	**Habits**
Eyes	**Last Seen**
Body Length	**Reward**
Height	

The
Call of the Wild

By Jack London